W9-CFQ-392

Night Catch

Brenda Ehrmantraut

Illustrated by Vicki Wehrman

ISBN 0-9729833-9-2

Library of Congress Control Number 2004099717

Designed by Richard Wehrman
Printed in the United States of America

Bubble Gum Press
416 4th Street SW
Jamestown, ND 58401

To order additional copies please go to:
www.bubblegumpress.net

For Cory, Parker & Drew
A soldier and his sons
~ *B. E.*

To my parents, Mel & Bea
and my children, Aaron & Aricia
~ *V. W.*

A soldier hugged
his son goodbye
and said,
"I'll miss you little guy."

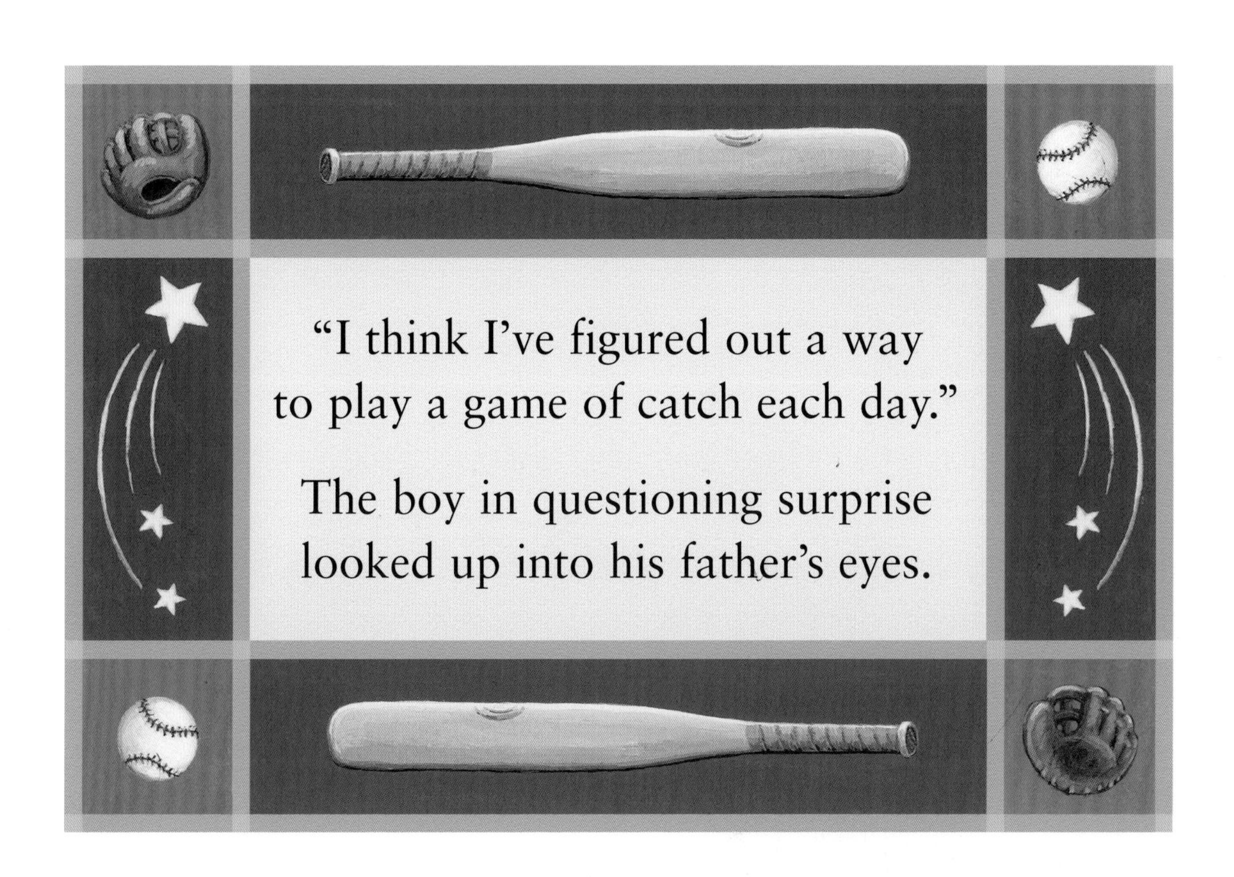
"I think I've figured out a way
to play a game of catch each day."
The boy in questioning surprise
looked up into his father's eyes.

“Not ball as usual in the park,

but something special after dark."

The dad continued with his plan,
“Think of this my little man.

The world is big and round
and wide. I’m going to the
other side.”

"Earth spins to face the
blazing sun then spins
some more 'til day is done.

So when one side
is hushed with night
the other side is
bathed in light."

"Because my night
will be your day,
we can play
our game this way:

Before you climb in bed each night, find Polaris shining bright."

"Breathe in deep, then blow out hard
to send that North Star
sailing far."

"Then close your eyes and have sweet dreams
of playing catch amid moonbeams.

The star will travel all the night
while you are sleeping, tucked in tight."

"I'll work while waiting patiently
for that North Star to come to me.

Then as you open up your eyes
I'll spot it in my darkening skies."

"I'll catch that star with a grand salute
on my end of its nightly route."

CEMBER

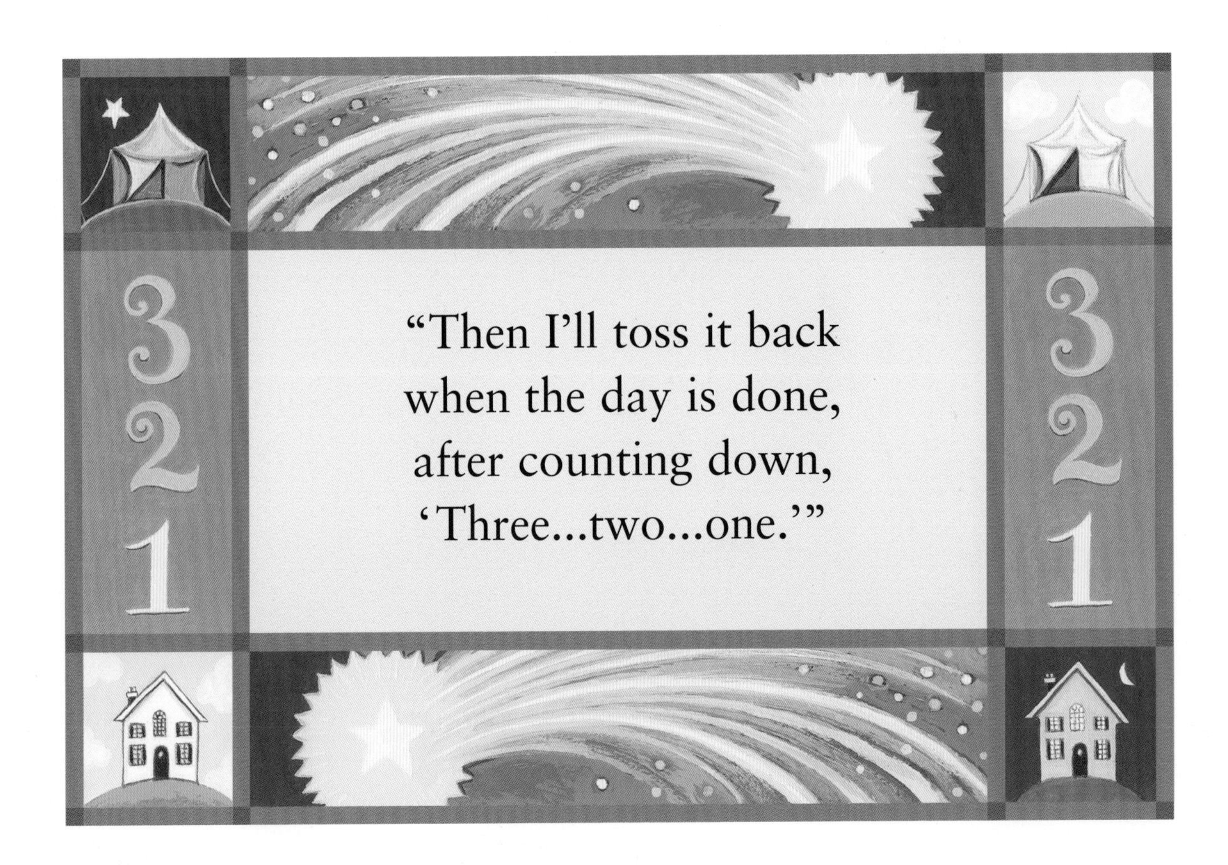

"Then I'll toss it back
when the day is done,
after counting down,
'Three...two...one.'"

"Back and forth our star will fly

racing through the nighttime sky."

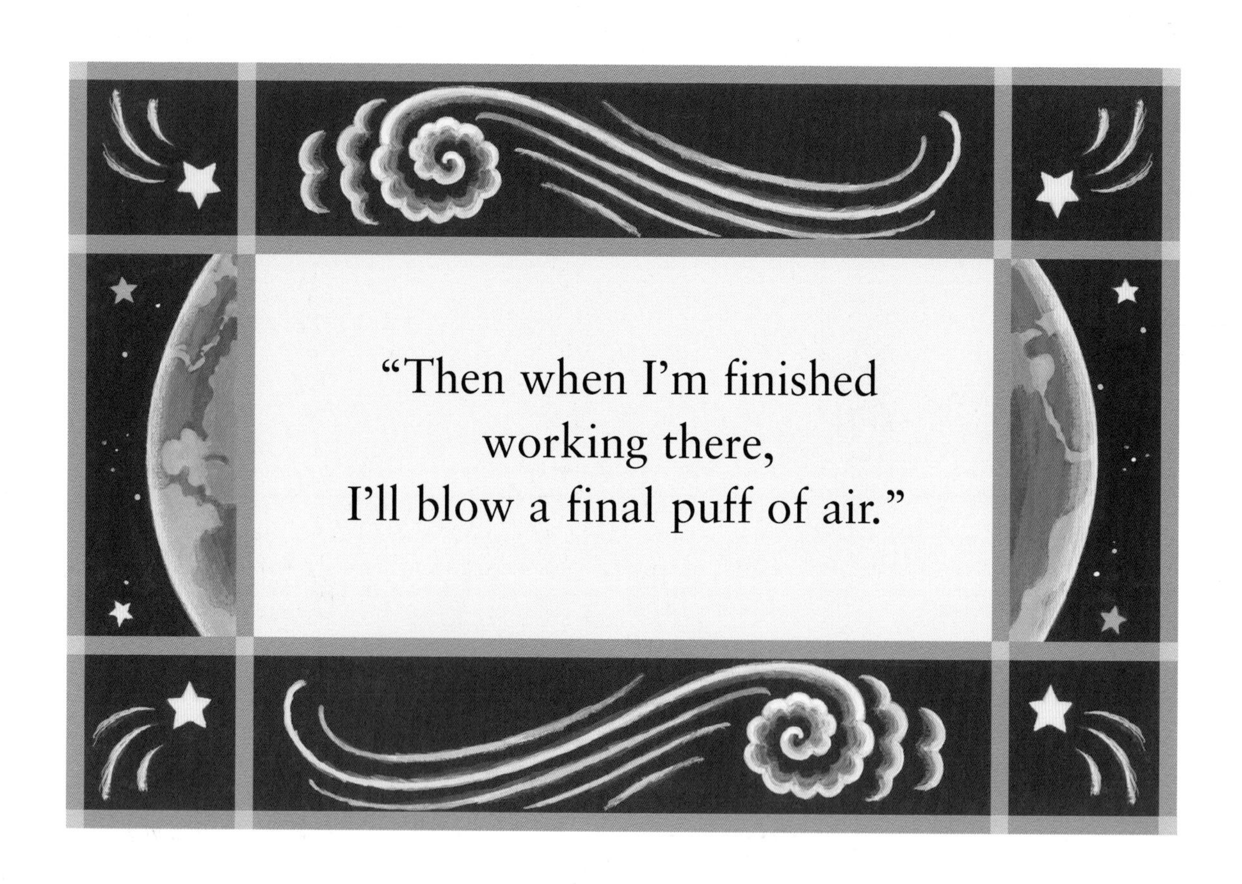

“Then when I’m finished
working there,
I’ll blow a final puff of air.”

"I'll board the plane and ask the crew
to race that star right back to you."

Polaris is another name for the North Star. Its place is directly over the North Pole. If the stars are shining, you can see Polaris from anywhere in the Northern Hemisphere, the top half of the world.

Some people think that the North Star is the brightest star in the sky, but really it isn't. Actually, it can be a little hard to spot. There is a trick for finding it, though, using star patterns called constellations.

The North Star is part of the Little Dipper, but you might spot it more easily by starting with the Big Dipper. The Big Dipper is a group of seven stars shaped like a scoop. Pretend it is a dot-to-dot picture. Begin at the bottom front star, draw an imaginary line toward the top front star and keep on going. That line will come very close to touching Polaris – The North Star!

Polaris
Little Dipper
Big Dipper

Here's a place for a picture of someone special